The Centurion

Books by HENRY TREECE

THE SPLINTERED SWORD
THE CENTURION

The Centurion

by HENRY TREECE

Illustrated by
MARY RUSSON

Meredith Press   New York

Library of Congress Catalog Card Number: 67-16509

MANUFACTURED IN THE UNITED STATES OF AMERICA FOR MEREDITH PRESS

VAN REES PRESS • NEW YORK

Contents

Introduction

ROMANS were some of the best soldiers the world has ever known. By the time of Jesus their Empire stretched right across Europe and into the Holy Land. In the year 55 B.C. Britain was first invaded by Julius Caesar, but a permanent settlement was not established until 43 A.D., when Roman legions came to Britain and fought the fierce Celtic tribes who lived there. Soon these Britons were defeated, and the Romans began to build fortress-cities and straight roads to keep the country in order.

This story is about a Roman. Once he had been a leader of soldiers in Britain and had commanded a hundred men. So he was a *centurion,* and the regiment he fought for was called the Ninth Legion. There were over six thousand Romans in it, many of them from Spain, which was a part of the Roman Empire.

When the story begins, in the year 61 A.D., Romans had been in Britain for nearly twenty years. By this time our Roman centurion was past the age of fighting. So the government of Rome, called the *Senate,* had given him a pension and a farm to live on.

But just when he had settled down to work peacefully as a

middle-aged farmer, something terrible happened. A British queen called Boudicca (or Boadicea) was very badly treated by some stupid Roman tax collectors. In revenge she raised an enormous army from among the tribes of the East Midlands, and then attacked every Roman she could find. She destroyed various cities held by the Romans, including London. Altogether her army killed seventy thousand Romans and their servants and friends.

Without any warning, the Roman centurion-farmer of this book found himself in the middle of this terrible war. What happened to him you will have to find out for yourselves.

As for Boudicca, she poisoned herself, rather than be taken prisoner, when her army of rebels was at last ambushed and destroyed by the Roman general, Suetonius.

As you read this story you will come across a number of new words. Do not let them bother you, because you will understand the story anyway. But if you feel like finding out exactly what these new words mean, there is a list of them at the back of the book. Read them when you feel like it—they are all very easy.

PART ONE

1

The Parting

THE gray stone square at Lindum Colonia echoed with the harsh shouts of soldiers. "Hail, Drucus Pollio!" they shouted. "Hail, and farewell!" They beat the long shafts of their javelins against their iron shields again and again. The noise they made frightened the white doves from the red roof of the temple to Mithras that lay beside the square. The birds fluttered up into the sunshine and, after a while, came down again to settle on the oak stockade where the Ninth Legion kept its horses tethered.

"Hail, Drucus Pollio," the red-faced men shouted again. "Hail, Centurion of all centurions! Hail!"

In the shade, under a red-striped awning, a man with short-cropped grayish hair wiped his left hand over his mouth and coughed, as though he was used to such shouting every day, as though the sound of men cheering meant nothing to him.

But the other tall dark man in the gilded armor and the high-crested helmet, who stood before him on the white steps, knew better. He said, "Go on, Drucus Pollio, wave your hand to them. Do not be ashamed; they deserve your salute as much as you deserve their cheers. Go on, Centurion."

3

Drucus Pollio half turned and nodded his cropped head to the massed legionaries. Then he forced himself to wave, as though with a great effort, and he smiled. For a time the square was silent; then, when the men saw that they had got to the heart of the old veteran, their shouts rang out wildly over the rolling green British countryside.

Quintus Petillius Cerialis, the legate of the legion in Lindum, watched. He bunched up his thin shoulders under the gilded armor and actually allowed his stiff face to smile. He said, "Well, Drucus, my friend, we have made you do something

4

our way at last! We have even got a smile out of that stone
face of yours! The Ninth Legion has not been defeated."

The centurion turned and stared at his commander. His
leather face had gone back into its usual lines. He said solidly,
"I do not see why I should smile and wave to men I have
barked at for thirty years, Legate. I am leaving the legion, at
the end of my service—as is the normal thing with officers of
my age. The Senate in Rome has offered me a little house and
farm in the district, and a decent pension to live on. I have
already written my thanks to the Senate. Now I have waved

and smiled at the men. Is there any other thing you would like me to do before I go?"

The legate gazed at him for a long while, calm-faced and unsmiling. Then he said gently, "Drucus Pollio, you and I are Romans born and bred; we ask no mercy and give no mercy. We are in Britain to do the work that our emperor commands us to do. But frankly, old friend, between ourselves, let us be human. Let us forget the army and the drill. Let us speak with one another as though we were of the same breed, and not as though we belonged to different races."

Drucus Pollio smiled again, distantly, then bowed his cropped head. "General," he said, "when I took the oath to serve the emperor and Rome, I did not promise to be human. We Romans do not expect to be human. We are fighting men, empire-getters, roadmakers. But, for this last time, I will forget all that. What shall we do?"

Quintus Petillius Cerialis froze a little in his splendid armor. Then, lifting the tall-crested helmet from his head, he said, "Let us go to my quarters and sit together for a little while before we part, old friend. Just a little while. Then—who knows —we may not see each other again, in this strange island."

So the two men went down the dim corridor and then into a small stone cell of a room where the only comforts were a plain wooden table and two leather-thonged stools. And there they sat facing one another while a Celtic slave girl poured some thin wine into the clay cups they held. And the legate said at last, "Old friend, you have seen many things. You have fought up and down the world, from Palestine to Germany. You have seen brave soldiers come and go, sometimes suddenly. More suddenly than they expected, perhaps. And now, at the end of your service with the Ninth, I am watching you go— quietly and without any blood being shed—to take up the farm and the pension that is your due. Let us drink to that."

Drucus Pollio put the cup to his lips and sipped at the tart wine, as the custom was. He said in a low voice, "I wish that your command of the Ninth may always be lucky, General. I wish that when you ride out the enemy falls back before your spears. That is the best I can wish."

The general looked at him for a time, then said, "Centurion, oh, Centurion. If you only knew, my old comrade. If you only knew . . ."

Drucus gazed at him quickly and said, "If I knew what, General? What more is there to know?"

But the legate did not answer.

Then Drucus gathered his armor and weapons and vinewood staff and handed them in at the legionary stores, as was the proper thing to do. The quartermaster there said, with a wry smile, "You'll soon be coming back for this lot, Centurion."

Drucus said solidly, "What, me? You must be insane, fellow. I have served my time. I have built fortresses where there was only ice before. And fortresses where there was only sand before. I shall not come back to Lindum."

The quartermaster took in the armor and weapons. He did not answer the veteran. He knew better than that. But, to a young British boy who helped in the store, he said, "That one is sure to come back. Rome never had a better soldier. He can only come back, with the trouble that is brewing. Where else is there for a Roman to go, in this damp, fogbound piece of island?"

But though the British boy did not know, Drucus Pollio knew. He went to the cell-like quarters of his oldest friends, the centurions Calgacus and Vitalis. They stood waiting for him, and Vitalis said, "Why, they said you had already left."

Drucus answered firmly, "How could I leave the Ninth without saying farewell to you two, Vitalis?"

So they went inside and spoke together by the little charcoal fire.

2

Three Old Soldiers

THE three centurions sat by the brazier. They were not very old in years, but all told, they had seen what there was of the world. They had been in the dark-green forests of Germany, the parched yellow land south of Alexandria, and up into the sky-floating blue rocks of the Pamir Mountains.

They had seen brown wolves, camels, and screaming eagles. They had eaten sheep and antelope, and even hawk, at a pinch.

They were brothers beside the brazier that threw its copper-bronze glow along the gray stone wall of the barrack block in windswept Lindum.

"Well, I am going, friends," Drucus Pollio said. "My time is up. It has been a good life, in a way. I am still alive."

Calgacus said, squinting out of his one eye, "When I signed on in Gaul, they said in my village that I wouldn't last a year with the legions. But see, I lost an eye outside Pylus from a chance slingstone; otherwise, I am perfect in wind and limb. Rome is not such a bad mistress to serve. A soldier gets a pension at the end."

And Vitalis said, "I swing my right leg a little, from that

arrow caught in the Sweetwater Canal by Alexandria. It never should have happened, but at the time I was only a young decurion and took a pride in being first at the attack. A young Arab girl dressed my wound with sheep's fat and herbs. She got me walking again in five days. I swore to marry her when the war was over. She was very pretty, with big, shiny black eyes like a gazelle."

Drucus Pollio said with a snort, "They are all like that, out there. Black hair and gazelle eyes. They all play the lute or the flute. And all Romans have sworn to come back and marry them since time began. I get bored with the tale."

Calgacus said, "You'll get even more bored, in a few weeks, on your little farm, ploughing this sad British clay, scattering the dry seed, waiting for it to come up again, then trying to get your lazy British slaves to put the sickle to it for bread when the harvest ripens. If it ever does ripen, in this slow, damp climate."

Vitalis laughed and rubbed his stiff right knee thoughtfully. Then, in a quiet voice, he said, "Our time will be up in a month, Calgacus. What shall we do then, try to scratch a living out of this British soil, or go down to Camulodunum and pass the rest of our days with other veterans of the legions?"

Calgacus shrugged his shoulders and said, almost sadly, "If I had been a careful saver all my time in the army, and had a bag of good money in my hand, I would do neither. I would buy a passage on a ship and go back to a little village I used to know, just north of Ostia. I can picture it now, with its white houses and the cypresses waving in the gentle sea breezes above the garden walls. When I was a boy, driving the black goats past those gardens, I used to dream of the time when I would be rich and have such a place. But I never shall now; it is only a dream. Thirty years with the Ninth, marching and fighting up and down Europe, leaves a man poorly prepared for a gentle, lazy life among flowers and cypress trees."

Drucus slapped him on the back. "You would die of boredom in a year, up above Ostia, old friend," he said smiling. "A hard-handed soldier, such as you are, must keep on working, at one thing or another, or he would just rust away like an unused sword. Take my advice and, when you leave the legion, get yourself a small farm somewhere up here on the wold. Keep yourself busy, keep your mind occupied with your crops and cattle and building."

Vitalis nodded. "You talk good sense, comrade," he said. "That's what we will do, Calgacus and I. We'll farm together, for company, and once in a while we'll all meet at the markets and fairs and do a bit of bargaining together."

Drucus said dryly, "Then you had better watch out, because I mean to become a sharp farmer. You will get no bargains from me, I can promise you."

They laughed and shook hands beside the brazier; then Drucus turned and went from the room without looking back. He was halfway down the dim corridor when a messenger came running up to him and said, "Sir, I am glad I caught you before you left. The legate would like to speak to you again before you set off. There is something more he wishes to say."

Drucus clucked with annoyance, but when he saw the serious look on the general's face, he said, "What is the matter, sir?"

Petillius Cerialis said slowly, "Drucus, I can no longer give you orders, but will you take my advice?"

The centurion smiled. "It depends on what the advice is, sir," he said.

Petillius came around the table and put his hand on the centurion's shoulder. Looking him in the eye, he said, "I advise you to go to the veteran's colony at Camulodunum and spend the rest of your days there."

Drucus shook his head. "I have been there once," he said. "It is full of old men who sit round the fire talking about the battles they were in. They live in a dim world of memories, sir. Their real lives stopped when they left the legion, and now they are only ghosts. Why, I would be a ghost myself if I went to Camulodunum. I doubt that I should live for more than a year."

The legate half turned from him and said in a low voice, "And if you go out into this wild country to start the farm you dream of, you may live less than a year."

Drucus asked sharply, "What do you mean, sir? I do not understand."

Petillius answered slowly, "I cannot say that I understand, either, my friend. All I can tell you is that the scouts have come in with rumors, picked up from various villages among the eastern tribes. Something is happening that I do not like. I can't put my finger on it exactly, but there is unrest among the tribes. They are disturbed about something or other. The young warriors are restless; the old men are silent and will not say what is happening. I tell you, Drucus, I do not like it."

The centurion nodded and smiled. "I have seen this happen before, sir," he said. "These British are a touchy lot. They listen to their druids and rainmakers, who live in a world of dreams and omens. It makes the young men restless, it gets them excited. But, in the end, all this unrest dies down and the tribes go on as they have always done. Don't forget, sir, they have no weapons these days. We collected all the swords and spears and axes when we made that sudden sweep down the eastern territory three years ago. Here, at Lindum, we have a garrison of six thousand trained soldiers, fully armed, and with a cavalry detachment. Even if the tribes flared up, for whatever reason, the Ninth could quiet them inside a week."

The legate sat down on his thonged stool, his head in his hands. He said wearily, "Drucus, it is not as easy as you think. I do not want to lead the Ninth out of Lindum to kill these young tribesmen. Romans are here in Britain to civilize them, not kill them. Besides, I am not sure that we should have such an easy time as you think, attacking them. They have weapons,

I know that. Only last week the chief's house at Ratae caught fire during one of their feasts. Our spy there reported that in the roof-thatch there were more than fifty good swords hidden."

Drucus slapped his hard hand on the table and said, laughing, "I know the chief you speak of, sir. He is no enemy to Rome; he is just a forgetful old man. He has a herd of a hundred horses to see to, and almost as many brothers, sisters, children, and grandchildren. I would guess that his mind was so filled with these other things, he had forgotten that the swords had ever been put up there."

Petillius answered coldly, "Sometimes I think that you are more British than the British, Drucus. How long have you served here?"

The centurion said, "Sixteen years, all but three months, sir. In that time, a man gets to know the tribes. I can speak to them in four different dialects. I know the names of their children, and who is married to whom. I have no fear of the tribes, Legate. I will take my chance and settle down on a farm among them."

Petillius rose from his stool and held up his hand in farewell. "May Mithras guard you, then, Centurion," he said. "I can do no more."

3

The Farmstead

TWO days' good marching south of Lindum, and three miles to the west of the straight military road that the Ninth had built, the Ermine Street, Drucus Pollio flung back the hood of his cloak, set down his walking staff and linen food bag, and laughed in the sunshine at what he saw.

Set among the rolling countryside was an even space, not too overgrown with dock and thistle, where a busy man could make four fields of wheat. In the middle of it was a stretch of well-drained chalk where a villa and barns could stand, their timbers untouched by rising damp.

Drucus strolled over to this place and said to himself, "A white villa with a red roof, and doves purring to one another along the ridge. Yes, that's what I want. And a little garden to grow herbs in, surrounded by cypresses. Traders bring cypresses into the port at Londinium, strong trees, half grown. I could have a score of them brought up here on the wagons that bring the food supplies to Lindum. Yes, and laurels. They could be brought from the Sicilian merchant ships. They would remind me of home. Laurels would flourish as well in this land as they do anywhere else, I would guess."

He wandered about this stretch of land. To the east there was a dense patch of woodland, never cleared by any man. Tall oaks, thick hawthorn, and spiked holly all grew there in abundance.

Through gaps in the trees, he could see the high wolds that stood between him and the distant sea. He said, "This wood can stand where it is. I shall not disturb it. It will keep off the east winds and protect the villa. Mithras gave me this wind-break!"

A little way into the wood there was a steep-sided valley covered with gorse and foxgloves. At the bottom ran a clear stream, flashing and rippling in the shafts of sunlight that came down between the oak boughs.

"Perfect!" said Drucus, aloud. "Quite perfect. This stream would water a thousand cattle. Where else on this earth could a simple man have found himself such a place to end his days in? Truly, the hand of the god has been held above me to protect me. Drucus, my man, you could never have chosen such a spot by yourself. You are too stupid. The hand of Mithras is concerned in this."

He was still laughing at his good fortune when from behind him he heard a cough. He swung round and there, in the thinnest part of the woodland, he saw an old man on a shaggy gray pony staring down at him. Behind this man stood five youths, carrying long spears and wearing leather helmets bound with bronze strips. They all wore cloaks of various shades of green. They stood as still and silent as leopards.

The old man on the pony wore a hood and cloak of goatskin, but the gold ring round his neck and the long coral-hilted sword across his thin thighs showed him to be a chieftain. His hair was long and white. His beard reached down over his chest. His close-set gray eyes, above a thin hawklike nose, seemed to measure and weigh everything he gazed at.

Drucus smiled at him and raised his right hand, open, to

show that he carried no knife. He said, "Greetings, old one. I am looking for a farmstead to settle on. This seems to be the place."

The old man stared on silently for a while, then he turned and nodded to the warrior-youths. They ran back into the wood. Then he kicked his gray pony a little closer to Drucus and said, "You have chosen wisely, Centurion. This is a good place. The fields raise good barley, the house site is well drained, the wood is a windbreak, and the stream waters the cattle."

Drucus laughed and said, "Those were my own thoughts, Chieftain. How did you know?"

The old man did not laugh. He said in his stiff voice, "It is my duty to know everything that happens in a part of the land where by fathers have farmed for two hundred years. That is what a chieftain is for, to know what is best. My own father lived here once, Drucus Pollio; until your people moved him onto the reserve near the garrison at Lindum, where he died of grief."

Drucus said, "I am sorry, Chieftain."

But the old man waved his words aside. "I do not ask pity from Romans," he said. "Or from anyone. Life is not a gentle pastime. But I can tell you that the place you choose for your house is the right place. No damp rises there. That is important in Britain, where most of us suffer from the damp-sickness that locks our bones. We had our house there until we were moved by the Roman Senate. You will not find traces of it now; the soldiers burned it down very thoroughly, then got slaves to plow the ashes into the soil. Only dock and willow herb now grow on that soil. I do not grieve. It is yours, if your Senate says so. I have my own house on the reserve, watched over by your own soldiers. I pay my taxes, small as they are. So, they protect me, the Romans—though there is no one to protect me from, except other Romans. I am satisfied. Whether my five sons will be satisfied when I have gone, that is for them to decide. Young men often have different thoughts from their father."

Drucus went up to the pony and stroked its gray muzzle. He had been in Britain long enough to know that a stranger did not tangle himself too deeply in an argument too soon. Instead, he said, "I thought I would grow wheat here, Chieftain."

The old man snorted, then said, "We grew barley. You are a soldier, not a farmer. Our barley was always good. It was the best south of Lindum. The other tribes admired our barley."

Drucus bowed his head before the old man, then said, "Right, in one field I will grow barley. In the other three, wheat."

Then the old chieftain laughed in the sunlight and said, "You are a Roman. I will come down to you."

Drucus held the pony's halter while the old man got down. Then together they went to a flat stone and sat. The old man said, "In truth, this is only moderate barley soil. Wheat would do much better. You are a wise man, only to give one field to barley. I admire a wise man."

Drucus did not answer just then, but watched silently as the five young men came out of the wood, beating a group of other men before them. Their wrists were tied with thongs, and they were clothed only in rags or pieces of old hide.

Then Drucus said quietly, "What have they done?"

The chieftain shrugged his thin shoulders and looked away. After a while he said, "Some are of my own folk, who broke the tribal law. Others are from away to the west, youths captured in raids. They are all slaves now."

Drucus said in a whisper, "You understand that it is against the Roman law for you to sell slaves? You are given a place on the reserve, you are protected by Rome. You cannot sell slaves as well."

For a time the old man did not answer. He began to polish

the smooth bright bronze of his old sword, whistling gently as he rubbed his cloak edge along it.

At last he turned, smiling, to Drucus and said, "I am not selling slaves, Centurion. I intend to execute them here, above the stream, where my family farmed for many generations. If you will kindly move back toward your military road, I will do what has to be done. There is no law against carrying out our own form of execution, as far as I have been told. Please go now."

Drucus rose and said firmly, "You cannot do this. I wish to farm here. How could I farm, with the thought of these dead ones always in my mind?"

The old chieftain smiled up at him and said, "Do not ask me, Centurion. I can tell you which crop to grow. I cannot tell you what you should think. That is your own Roman business, not mine."

Then he looked past Drucus and called out to the five sons in a language that the centurion could not understand. The youths began to thrash the slaves toward the flat stone where the two men had been sitting. The first of the slaves was a dark-eyed man whose tribal cheek-scars showed that he had once been a warrior. He walked firmly, though they pushed and beat at him. And when he was near the stone, Drucus said to him, "Can you speak Roman, man? Should I buy you? What do they call you?"

The dark-eyed man looked up at Drucus and smiled gently. Then, in good Latin, he said, "I am named Dio, after a Roman friend of my father. But you should not buy me unless you buy the others as well. I would not want their deaths in my dreams. It is up to you."

Then he turned away and nodded to the nearest warrior, as though he were ready to bend his head over the flat stone.

But Drucus sprang forward and shouted, "Stop! I will buy them, even if it takes the last of my pension. No farm would thrive on such bloodshed."

There was a great silence then. The warriors stared at Drucus, and the slaves gazed down at the ground. The old chieftain put his long sword on the stone and took the centurion by the sleeve.

"Step a little way with me," he said. "I do not wish all the world to hear what I say."

And when they had paced twenty yards, the man said, "That Dio is a good fellow. You can trust him to the last. Young Simia is a bit flighty, but he will learn, in good time. As for the others, they need training. But you will know all about that, having been in that business for so long."

Drucus said stiffly, "What price do you ask?"

The old chieftain grinned up at him, then smacked him quite hard on the shoulder. "No price at all, Roman," he said. "I have got your measure now. If I asked a price, I would be up before the legate in a week's time, and due for the cells in Lindum. All my sons would be foot soldiers in the Ninth, as well. No, Drucus Pollio, the slaves are yours. I have met a harder bargainer than myself, and I know it."

But Drucus was still uncertain. He said calmly, "Very well, Chieftain. I take them as my farm workers. What do you want for them that might not put you in the cells and your sons in the legion?"

The old man said smiling, "Give me that belt you wear, with the Roman buckle shaped like an eagle's head. That would satisfy me."

Drucus took off the belt. He said, "I gained that in a battle, outside the city of—"

But the old man waved him to silence. "I do not want to know," he said. "It is a pretty belt. Good day to you, and may your farm thrive."

Drucus watched them go across the wold, stirring the dust behind him, without another farewell. Then Dio came up to him smiling and said, "Very well, master, where shall we begin to build your farm?"

PART TWO

4

Lavender Garden

Drucus was digging in his garden, moving his broad shoulders with the easy swing of a soldier trained in the use of sword and shield. The afternoon sun glinted on the metal of his spade; it was as well kept and polished as a javelin point.

He paused after a while and wiped the sweat from his brown forehead with the back of a gnarled square hand. Then he loosed the belt of his leather tunic a little and smiled to himself.

"Drucus Pollio," he whispered, "nearly thirty years a centurion of the First Cohort, Ninth Legion! Well, Drucus Pollio, you haven't done badly for yourself after all. A villa within reach of the Ermine Street; four rich fields of grain; three black horses—and a pension solid enough to let you live out your days in decent comfort. No, not bad for the son of a water carrier from Tarraco! Not bad at all."

He gazed past the white-painted villa surrounded by cypresses where doves purred on the red-tiled roof, and toward the far field where five slaves, their yellow hair bound up, swung sickles at the amber-headed wheat and sang a slow mournful song.

To himself he said, "Ah, these Britons! They take their time

about it! If I had only married, if I had only got a son or two to
stir these fellows up, then harvesting would be no problem.
But there it is—the Ninth Legion was my wife, my sons, and
my mother. Now I am old."

He shrugged his shoulders and bent at his digging once
more. He was planting a bed of lavender to lie just beyond a
marble balustrade he had set up. He knew that lavender was
no sort of thing for a horny-handed soldier who had stood
under the whining arrows at Camulodunum and slept in the
white snowdrifts at Caer Caradoc—but he had always wanted
a bed of lavender. It reminded him of the winding hill path
just on the edge of the brown desert outside Tarraco when he
was a boy. In those days, walking with his two sisters, he had
often plucked the wild lavender that grew between the rocks,
and had bruised its leaves between his fingers for the little
girls to smell its bitter-sweetness. Now, after all those weary
years, he was planting lavender of his own, in the garden of
his own farmhouse, so that he could bring back the past when-
ever he wished. And that is very often for a man who stands on
the doorstep of old age without any laughing sons to follow
him.

All at once things went very quiet. The songs in the far field
had stopped. Even the sighing of wind in the grain and the
lazy buzzing of bees had stopped. All that Drucus could hear
was the creaking of his own leather belt and the clink of his
iron spade as it struck upon a stone.

He straightened up and stared toward the wheatfield, thinking that he would tell that foreman-slave Dio there would be
no black bean soup for supper unless more work was done. But
the slaves were not there any longer. The field was empty.

Drucus Pollio stuck his spade into the earth and said, "By
Mithras and the seven lights! But I'll know the reason for this!"

He had only taken two steps in the direction of the house
when a group of men came around the gable wall and ran

toward him. From their red and blue shirts he could tell that they were Coritani from the tribal reserve just south of Lindum. But these young men carried axes and hay-knives, and they came at him like hounds at a wolf.

Drucus Pollio put on his parade-ground face and said sharply, "Well, my lads, and what is all this? Since when does your chief let you run about with eagle's feathers in your hair and that ridiculous blue warpaint daubed all over your faces?"

They did not answer him, but still rushed on. When they were within three paces, their leader, a tall boy with plaited black hair, began to shout in a high, cracked voice and to strike out with a curved sword made from a broken scythe-blade. Drucus swayed to let the blow pass him, then sent the youth staggering back with a hard thump on the chest.

The others stopped and glared at the old soldier like house dogs who have cornered a badger and do not know what to do with him next.

Drucus Pollio's face was red with anger. He said, "What is all this? Have you no work to do? Are there no sheep to watch over? What have you against me to come picking a quarrel in the harvest season? Come on, you understand camp Latin as well as I do; speak up. None of that gabbling of yours now. Speak up!"

The black-haired youth shouted harshly, "It is over. That time is over. You are dead."

Drucus Pollio half turned away from them and tensed both his arms. Then he said with a smile, "I can assure you I am very much alive, my friends. If you doubt it, then come and try for yourselves. Now what is this about? Who has upset you?"

For a while he let his light-gray eyes wander over their dark faces. Some of them glared back at him, but at last they all looked away. Then Drucus saw one among them that he knew.

"Now then, Keromac," he said, "aren't you the fellow I found lying in the stream bed with a broken leg last year? The time your horse trod on you and bolted? Is this what I get for putting your leg in splints and sheltering you for a month? Come on, man, let me hear your voice again. You were not backward at talking when I knew you then."

Keromac shuffled his feet and looked down at the dust. Then he said, "Yes, you looked after me, Centurion."

Drucus Pollio said evenly, "Give me my name, Keromac, as I give you yours. Your chief teaches you politeness, doesn't he? Very well, now tell me what you are up to, leaving your work at harvest time."

Keromac suddenly pushed his knife into his belt and said, "Drucus Pollio, we are driving out the Romans. They have made slaves of us, but now we are destroying them forever."

Drucus Pollio smiled at him out of half-shut eyes and said, "That should be interesting to watch, Keromac. When you boys with your garden tools see the cohorts in line with the sun on their shields, and when you hear the trumpets braying and the horses snuffling—yes, that should be interesting. And when do you propose to give us this entertainment, Keromac?"

The man looked the soldier in the eye and said almost gently, "It is already happening, Pollio. The Ninth has been ambushed and cut up. Half of them lie along the Ermine Street; the other half are battering at the gates of Lindum and screaming to be let in."

Drucus Pollio picked up his spade and dug another spit of soil as though the men were not there. Then he turned and said, "Yes, yes, Keromac. And in Rome the Emperor Nero has packed up all his belongings and has fled to Parthia in terror. Is that it?"

Keromac said seriously, "Not yet, Pollio, but that too will happen."

The soldier leaned on his spade and laughed. "I can take a joke as well as most men. Now be off with you all and let me get on with something important."

The black-haired leader walked up, stiff-legged like a dog, and stood beside Drucus. "You Romans will not believe that there is a storm until the thunderbolt strikes you down, will you? Very well, I tell you that there is a great rising. The country is on fire. All the tribes are out. We are nothing, we few, but behind us comes a great army, led by the Queen." He began to wave his arms about wildly.

Then Keromac came forward and said, "We have pledged ourselves to Boudicca of the Iceni, Pollio, and she is leading us to victory. If you would like to hear it, I will tell you the names of five centurions and thirty decurions who fell outside Lindum. Perhaps you will remember some of them. Certainly you will know the names of Calgacus and Vitalis—veterans like

yourself? They lie in their gardens now, only a mile away, staring at the sky."

Drucus Pollio felt very tired. He pushed his spade into the ground and shook his head as though trying to forget. He said, "Very well, let me walk into my house for the last time. You can finish me there as well as out here. I have a right to die in my own place where I am the master."

But Keromac suddenly put his hand on the Roman's shoulder and said, "A life for a life, Pollio. I would have died a year ago if you had not found me in the valley. You are a good man, for a Roman. But our queen does not know that, and she is riding with her host to destroy Londinium. She will tread down your fields and turn your house to rubble. Accept my advice and leave before she comes. Take food and what clothes you can carry, and make your way through the woodland toward the sea. Go, and good luck to you."

Then, as Drucus gazed at them in astonishment, the band of young warriors turned and ran on through his farmland, never looking behind. He watched them for a time, then went slowly to the villa. In the cool dairy he packed a loaf of white bread and a goat-milk cheese into a bleached linen bag. Then he filled a skin with sharp red wine and slung it onto his back. From his cedarwood chest he took his warmest cloak of dark-blue wool, the old parade cloak that he had kept carefully since his discharge from the legion.

In the living room he glanced around for a moment at the stout furniture and the little mosaic set in the floor, showing the Ninth's war eagle made of yellow pieces of stone, surrounded by a laurel wreath.

Then he swung around abruptly and walked away from the place, and he did not stop until he reached the outlying stretch of woodland four hundred paces away. Among the oaks, the hawthorns, and holly he sat down on a moss-covered stone. A

hare came out of a clump of gorse to gaze at him with great blank eyes, but the Roman sat quite still until the puzzled animal grew tired of watching him and ambled away like a forgetful old man.

5

Red Queen

WHEN the wineskin was half empty and the beeches on the western wolds had turned from bronze to purple, Drucus Pollio sat up sharply and listened. The earth, his earth, granted to him by the legion and the Senate, shuddered with the tramp of feet and the rumble of solid-wheeled wagons. He stared through the dusk and saw his fields swarming with the dark shapes of many folk. There were countless banners and spear-points glistening. His keen ears even picked up the swishing cracking sound of wheat stalks breaking before this host. He remembered the pains he had been at to sow his seed, come all the way from Carthage in North Africa—a bag of silver the bushel—and he groaned with misery.

Later, when the fires started up in his courtyard and men began to sing and dance around the fishpond he had so laboriously built with his own hands, Drucus Pollio wrapped his blue cloak about his head and tried to shut out the noise.

Then, when the pale moon rode across the sky, he was aware of tall, stabbing red flames coming up from behind the villa.

"Mithras!" he said. "They have fired the stables!"

He got to his feet and went out from the wood into the nip-

ping air. Now he could not doubt it; his stables were ablaze. He even saw two men in shaggy skins whipping his horses away over the moorland with sticks, his black stallions that had cost him two years' pension money.

Drucus Pollio clapped his hard hand to his head. "Oh, Mithras," he said. "Oh, Lord of Light—how can you permit this?"

Almost before he knew what he was doing, he began to stride toward his house. Then that stride became a run, and soon he saw men lying on the pavement of his courtyard, spearing at the carp in his pool with sharpened willow sticks.

Fires were banked up here and there on the mosaics; youths were carelessly hacking at the marble pillars of his portico with their hatchets, just to pass the time.

Drucus Pollio thought that he would rather die than have such barbarism come back to the land.

"Hey, you," he called, "in the emperor's name, what has got into you? Is no man's house sacred?"

A great shape rose up from behind a laurel that Drucus had had brought from Sicily. It was a warrior wrapped in a black bear's pelt, his head all shaggy, his eyes glaring. Drucus saw the man's white teeth in the moonlight, and he punched him back to the ground before he could lift his ax.

Then the Roman ran on, gasping with tiredness. And when he passed through the gate of his own courtyard, he could have wept to see the ruin that the tribesmen had made of it all. There was a little gilded statue of Apollo set on a black basalt column he had prized. Now the head and the outstretched arms were gone, and the column itself was leaning sideways as though a great wind had wrenched it from its seating. "You savages!" he shouted. "If you will do this, how can you hope to be treated like men? Have you no decency?"

Four young Iceni jumped up and took him by the arms, laughing at his struggles, and hauled him away. They smelled of sweat and hide, and they overcame him so easily that he

35

wanted to die right then, recalling the time when he had stood
firm in Libya as the hosts of Tacfarinas had swept forward at
his cohort, humming like bees and waving their reddened
assegais.

Then suddenly he was flung onto the pavement and looked up
to see a woman above him, sitting in his own carved chair that
they had brought from the dining room. She was not a pretty
woman, being olive-skinned and squarely built, with a coarse
black mane that curled about her shoulders like writhing snakes.
But there was something about her that was queenly. It was not
the gold at her throat and arms, or the red cloth and fox furs
wrapped about her body. Her queenship lay in the firm brown
face streaked with white ash, and in the blue caste-spot, the
Eye of Diana, painted in the middle of her broad forehead.

She gazed down at Drucus as though he were a miserable dog
in the street below her chariot wheel and said, "Who speaks of
savages here? Who dares raise his voice before the queen?"

It was like kneeling before a leopardess in a dark cave, or
some untamed wild-haired priestess beside her smoldering altar
in a lonely forest. This queen was not like any woman Drucus
had seen before. She seemed more an animal goddess—who
hated all men, who ruled over lions and wolves and bears, and
who spoke the tongue of seals and falcons and was loved by
them.

Drucus came to his senses with great effort.

"Lady," he said, "I demand little in this hard life; but at least
I am entitled to ask for common justice. No queen would deny
me that."

Her nostrils pinched in hard; her thick lips drew themselves
to narrow lines. She waited a while, then said, "You—a Roman
—are entitled to nothing save a rope round your thieving neck.
To nothing save a bullock's death."

The old veteran drew in his breath and waited until his heart
beat a little slower. Then, as though he spoke to a chosen band

of his own soldiers, he said calmly, "I am the master of this house. I am Drucus Pollio, centurion of the First Cohort, Ninth Legion of Spain. I hold the Oak Leaf for things the god let me do on the ramparts at Glevum. I have the Bronze Eagle from Deva, awarded by the general, Suetonius himself. These things I mention not from pride but because you force me to declare myself. If this entitles me to a bullock's death, lady, then I am willing to leave such a world as this has grown into."

For a time there was silence. Even the Britons laughing by the fishpond were still, staring back to where this firm-voiced soldier dared to speak up to their queen.

Then Drucus saw the queen's feet coming down the steps toward him. She wore no sandals, and there was nothing to show the difference between this great lady and a slave. He looked up higher and saw her lips now smiling. She said slowly, in camp Latin, "Forgive me, warrior. In cases like this there are always mistakes. Get up from your knees and stand before me as the old Greeks used to do, praying to their god. Men like you are not born to kneel."

Drucus rose and looked her in the eye. "I am not fit to be

named among Greeks, lady," he said. "All I ask for is common justice. I am a soldier who has done his service, and I claim no more than the right to live quietly until the god calls me."

Boudicca looked at him with a long smile, her brown fingers playing with the gold snake about her neck. Then she said, as gaily as a young girl, "Forget the god, and think of the goddess. It is my opinion that you should set a higher value on yourself, soldier. In this world, there are many who carry swords, but there are few men. You are a man, sir."

Drucus felt bewildered by this and shrugged his shoulders. "I am a farmer now, lady," he said. "I have served my time and, by the grace of the emperor and the Senate, I am given a farm-

stead and a pension to run it. I ask for no more. But, I beg you, tell your people to leave my fishpond and statues alone. They have cost me good money and labor. It is the same with my fields. These things must be won, must be wrenched from the earth with pain and worry. I am no great nobleman with a host of servants to help me. What I have, I must work for. You see, my lady, I am a simple man who holds to the law, no more and no less."

Queen Boudicca said quietly, "I see that you should be a

captain among men, Roman. With such a general as you, I could bring my own feckless dogs to heel. I could march down to Londinium and set my heel on the vipers' nest there. And afterward, I could build ships and cross to Gaul, where I have many kinsfolk who would rise at my call."

She paused, then turned on the steps and put her hand to her painted forehead. At last she said, "Beyond Gaul lies Rome, where a smaller man than you, Centurion, strums on the lyre and calls himself God. Oh, Roman, what might we not do together, you and I! It is enough to make even your Jupiter laugh!"

Drucus was aware of the many eyes turned on him now from among the bright fires. He said stiffly, "Lady, your business is

your business. I am not concerned in it. If my grain from Carthage yields well, that is all I want from life. I do not wish for glory."

He was startled when the woman suddenly swung round and almost screamed, "Take him! Bind him! The man is a fool! He shall learn what it is to laugh in the face of a queen."

Then, all about him, he heard the buzzing of excited voices, as though he were the victim in the middle of a swarming hive.

6

Dawn Visitor

TWO young men in fur caps and stinking horsehides tied him with thongs and carried him into his own cold dairy. As they flung him onto the hard red tiles, one of them said, "She has commanded that when you have spent the night in suffering, one of us shall come back and give you her justice for your Roman pride. Pray well, Centurion, the dawn is not far away."

Then they left him, and he soon knew what it was to lie on his own cold tiles. It was almost as bad as the time when he had tried sleeping in the snow-capped Pennines alongside a young tribune of the Ninth called Petillius Aggravinus. He was a thin-faced youth with long, oiled hair, and a small mole on his right cheek. He had whimpered in his sheepskin bag as the wolves howled along the snowline; but when the time came, outside Eburacum, this tribune led the charge and overturned three chariots before he ended. Drucus thought of him now as he lay in the dairy and, among the scents of pressed cheeses and butter, came to the conclusion that you couldn't judge a man by his long hair or his beauty spots.

Outside, owls called from the trees, and the many small beasts of the fields cried out in warning as the white-winged hunters drifted. Drucus thought: There they are, trying to keep their precious little lives, under the hoverer. And here I am, already cold as death, waiting for the queen's justice. I, who was once the Elephant of the Regiment, shivering in my own dairy! Why, when I marched across the square at Lindum, new recruits from Germany and Egypt shook with palsy—and here I am, shaking myself, because the woman who leads these savages has threatened me. I will go to sleep and forget it all! I will not shiver like a frightened dog!

But he did not go to sleep. He stayed very wide awake, until dawn came down under the door and onto the cold floor. And when this happened, he heard a man's footsteps passing through the courtyard, and a high gay tune being whistled, as though the queen had sent a meadowlark to put an end to him.

The door swung open at last, and a young man stood there trying to get his blue eyes used to the dusk of the dairy, and tossing up a leaf-bladed bronze sword from hand to hand.

Drucus Pollio saw that the youth had tawny-reddish hair which curled round at the nape of his thick brown neck. The young man reminded him of someone, but he could not quite think who it was.

Then the visitor called out, "Are you all right, sir? You do not look too comfortable, lying where you are."

Drucus rolled on to his right side and growled, "I am well enough, Briton; how are you?"

The young man smiled pleasantly and pointed his sword at the centurion, as though taking aim before a run. "I?" he said, lightly. "I am well enough. It has been a cold march through the briers and the fields, but the larks are rising and the breezes are freshening, and it looks like a bright day. I am well enough, since you ask."

He came down the steps and sat beside Drucus on the floor, running his thumb along the keen blade of his sword and hissing between his teeth, as a groom does when he curries a horse.

Drucus said, "Well, that is good news, then."

The young warrior nodded. "It is always good news if one is alive to hear it," he said. "As for me, I am sent by Queen Boudicca with a message that might not be good news to the one who receives it."

Drucus ignored this and said, "You must be someone of note, to carry a queen's message, young man."

The Celt laughed. "I am her sister's son. I am Lydd Guletic, the prince," he said. "But you would not know it from the way the men treat me. All I have to show for it is my sword. See, it is an heirloom, made of the old bronze from Belgica. The haft

and blade are in one piece, not like the new swords of bone and
iron. Yet the balance is so perfect that this sharp blade would
scarcely stop a man from speaking as it separated his head from
his shoulders. I wish you were unbound; then you could test it
yourself."

Drucus said, "Yes, I wish I were unbound, too."

The young man gazed down at him for a while, then, pushing
the sword into his hide belt, he said, "Come, let us forget such
things for the moment. My walk has made me hungry, and no
doubt you will feel the same, lying on that cold floor. Why old
men like you choose to lie on cold floors when there are good
beds to be had, I shall never understand."

Drucus started to tell him, but Lydd Guletic waved his hand
and said, "I will light a fire and we will break our fast together
with warm porridge and mulled wine. Would that suit you?"

Drucus nodded his head. "That would suit me very well," he
answered.

Then, as he watched the young man blowing on the fire and
beating up the oat porridge in a clay bowl, he suddenly called

to mind whom the youth resembled—it was a nephew of his from Saguntum, along the coast south from Tarraco. This boy had been called Drucus Gallo, and had died when he was just sixteen outside the gates of Apulum in Dacia as a sudden hail of stones came over from the garrison catapults.

The centurion called out to Lydd, "Don't hold the porridge pan in the middle of the flames. It will turn out like burned oat-cakes that way."

The young man nodded and smiled. "Thank you," he said. "I have had little practice at this trade, you understand. All my life they have made me ride horses and swing swords. But I am learning."

When he came back with the porridge bowls, he set them on

the dairy floor and said, "Now here is a difficulty. You are tied up like a pig on the way to market and cannot use your hands. What shall I do, feed you with this horn spoon?"

Drucus said, "Your hands are shaking so much with the morning chill that I do not think you would get it into my mouth. And I would feel foolish with porridge dripping over my chin, at my age."

For a long moment the prince looked down at him unsmiling. Then he said quietly, "I see your problem, sir. But I too have a problem; I am sent by my kinswoman the queen to find a Roman who has offended her and to deal with him. Now I do not know who is who in these parts, but if you are not that Roman, then all I have to do is to cut your bonds and then we

can eat our breakfast together before I go on to hunt down this man. What do you say to that? *Are* you the Roman?"

For the space of five breaths Drucus Pollio was silent, then suddenly he looked above the young man's head and spoke.

7

Bronze Sword

YOU need search no further, Lydd," he said. "I am the man you have come to find. I cannot say that I fear either your sword or your queen. So carry out your orders now, while the morning sun is shining—and deal with me, as you put it."

Lydd Guletic looked down into the old centurion's eyes with his own cold blue ones, in a long stare. And as he stared he slowly drew the bronze sword. The russet light of morning glimmered along its pale-golden edge, and Drucus thought almost idly that if a man must die by the sword, this one was not an unworthy weapon to end on. Silently, without moving his lips, he made a little prayer to Mithras, Lord of Light, Slayer of Bulls. It was this:

"O Master, in the years you have allowed me I have marched many miles up and down the world. You have been generous enough to let me see many places and to talk with many men. Though I have committed errors, I can tell you honestly that I have always regretted what I have done wrong, and I have often tried to do right. I can assure you that I have never betrayed a friend. Now that my time is on me, my only plea to

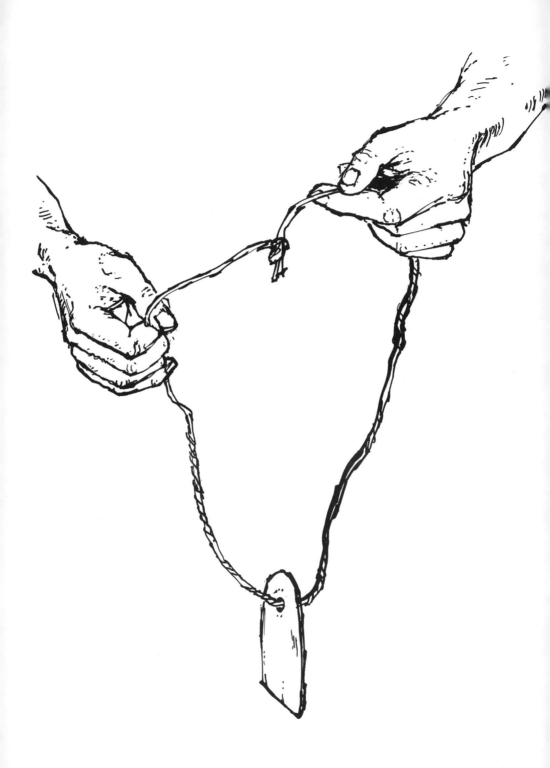

you is that I make a swift end and go to where I may once more meet the men I marched with."

And when he had said this, inside his head, he looked up at the Briton and nodded. Lydd Guletic raised the sword and brought it down with a sudden slash.

The hide thongs about the soldier's wrists fell away. Then the Briton bent again, and now the ankle trusses were cut through.

He placed the sword beside him on the red tiles and smiled. "Rise, my friend," he said. "You will catch your death of cold on those tiles."

Drucus Pollio stretched his shoulders and then began to rub his wrists where the thongs had bitten in. He said evenly, "You were commanded to deal with me, young man. Is this how you obey the orders of your queen?"

Lydd held a dish of steaming porridge toward him. "I have dealt with you in the way she would have wished, Roman," he said. "My queen admires brave men. She would not want such as you to vanish from the earth, since there are so few of you left among men."

He rose then and went to where his cloak and leather pouch lay on the steps. From the pouch he took a calfskin bag and a yellow bone tally on a knotted cord, such as herdsmen hang about the necks of sheep when they have bought them in the market.

Turning to Drucus, he said, "Here is a bag of coin—enough to buy you three farms. The queen sends it to you, partly to show that she is sorry to have spoiled your house, and partly to show you that she is more generous in her gifts than your fat emperor and miserly Senate in Rome."

Drucus set the bag beside him and went on eating his porridge. Lydd Guletic kneeled and placed the cord about the Roman's neck, so that the bone tally hung upon his chest. "This

is the queen's sign," he said. "No one will harm you while you are wearing it, for all will know that she has chosen you as her friend."

Drucus finished off the last spoonful of porridge, then rose and stretched his arms and stamped his feet to get the warmth back into them. He said, "I may be a foolish old fellow whose wits have been dried up by too much marching under the sun and sleeping under the moon, but, to tell you the truth, I do not understand all this."

Lydd looked up from his bowl and smiled. "Few of us ever do, Centurion," he said. "All I can tell you is that the queen thought again about this matter after she and her army left your farmstead. Now if you had told me that you were *not* the Roman, such lying would not have pleased her. No, in my opinion, if you had lied to me, you would not be standing here talking to me now."

The Roman said gently, "You speak with a great deal of confidence, young man. Yet you are sitting with your back toward me and all I have to do is to bend and pick up your sword to put you in a very awkward position. Yes, a most awkward position."

Lydd Guletic did not look up. All he said was, "This porridge lacks sweetness. Now, among my tribe we mix the oats with the honey of wild bees before we pour milk upon them. It makes a great difference. You should try it, Centurion."

Drucus bent over and patted him on the shoulder, smiling. "For such a young man," he said, "you are full of good advice."

Lydd nodded and then wiped his lips. "I have still more advice for you," he said. "Soon everything will be changed here in Britain. There will be no legions, no taxgatherers—no centurions, even. All that you have known will disappear. Be ready for this change, old friend; go somewhere else to build your new

farm—to some place which the Romans have not mauled with their roads and walls and villas and fortresses. Go among the Demetae, the gentle people of the West. There you will be safe, and the good folk will respect you as a hard-working farmer."

But Drucus stood by the door now, looking across his fields and the woodland into the sun. He said, "I do not think so, friend. I do not wish to leave this place, where I built the walls with my own hands and I know every tree. No, thank your queen—but I shall stay here now. I am too old a dog to change my ways."

Lydd pushed his sword back into its sheath, then flung his heavy cloak over his left shoulder. He said, "You must please yourself, Centurion. That is your right as a man. But I know what I would do if I stood in your shoes."

Then he went up the three stone steps and stood for a moment sniffing the clean air of morning. The sunlight caught his tawny hair and made him look like a young lion.

For an instant Drucus almost wept to see him standing there in the golden light as though there were nothing in the wide world that could hurt him and humble him and destroy him. This was how his own nephew had stood, smiling up at the sun, before he fell under the ballistae outside the walls of Apulum in Dacia.

Bitterly now the Roman wished he had such a son. For one mad moment he almost ran after Lydd and put his arms about him. Then that moment passed, and the centurion's face became a parade-ground mask again. A soldier's life was all meeting, and then parting.

"Go with the god, young man," he said. "And may the luck of Mithras always ride on your sword-point."

The young man halted then and turned around, smiling. "It seems to me," he said, "that you have more need of luck than I,

Centurion. You, an old man living in a wilderness, with no sword
to guard you. Here, take my sword, the queen will see to it that
I am given another. With this at your side, a man like you will
never lack a friend."

Drucus would have loved to accept such a gift from this
young man, but he hardened his face and answered, "I cannot
take another man's sword, Lydd. The only weapons such as I
may bear must be given by my emperor."

He held his hands tightly clasped behind his back as he said this, so they would not betray him by reaching out. Lydd laughed again, then said, "As you wish, old man. But never forget that I made the offer."

Then he swung round and walked away, vaulting the balustrade and striding down through the wheat as though it were of no account. Drucus watched him for a long while, seeing him throw the sword into the sunlit air and then catch it again and again. The sound of his merry whistling kept coming back on the morning breeze almost until the youth was out of sight beyond the swaying beechwoods.

And when he had gone, Drucus punched his fist against the hard lintel of the door a time or two, then went off to see how he should set about building his stables once more.

8

New Roof

LATE that afternoon the runaway slaves came back, very sheepish and not daring to look Drucus in the eye. He did not reproach them for deserting him, for it was no part of a slave's duty to defend his master. Fighting was the task of freemen and trained soldiers.

All that Drucus said was, "There is much work to be done here now. We must cut roof timbers from the woods, fetch reeds from the stream bed, and haul stones from the quarry. There will be no time for singing and games until we have a safe house about us again."

Dio said, "What of the harvest, master? That is not yet in, and the rains may come before we expect them."

The Roman said sharply, "The god will take care of that, Dio. He has looked after us so far. He will not fail us now."

As he spoke, a chill wind blew across the stackyard, and a white owl suddenly broke from a cypress tree in full daylight and fluttered clumsily above the men's heads. Dio clapped his hands over his eyes and said, "Have mercy, Earth Mother, the Roman did not mean what he said."

Some of the other slaves sank to their knees and touched the ground with their foreheads. Drucus pursed his lips together and turned away from them. He did not want them to see his face.

"Get about your work, men," he said. "We still have three hours of light for tree felling and reed pulling."

Then he went into the shell of his house and sat at the cracked table with his head in his hands, suddenly feeling very old and lonely.

As dusk was falling, he heard the slaves returning, dragging their heavily laden cart to the house and singing one of their endless, monotonous work songs. Drucus thought: If I live in Britain for a hundred years, I shall never get used to this strange music of theirs. It is enough to drive a man out of his mind.

Then he heard footsteps shuffling across the paved floor toward him and looked up to see the slave Dio standing beside the table and holding out something in both his hands. The light had failed so quickly that Drucus could not see what it was.

"Well, Dio," he said, "have you brought something for me? What is it—a cow's horn or a bunch of harebells?"

He tried to laugh as he spoke, but the slave answered in a serious, slow voice, "It is a sword, master."

Drucus bowed his head now in the twilight, not daring to look up. At last he said to the waiting slave, "It is a bronze sword of your own people, is it not? The handle and the blade of one piece?"

Dio said in a gentle voice, "You have described it, master."

Then Drucus put his hands over his face for a while. "Where did you find it?" he asked.

The slave said, "By the stream, when we went to cut reeds for the stable roof, master. He who had owned it lay with his lion-colored hair in the water. You would have thought he was smiling, if you had seen him."

Drucus said, "Yes, I know. I have seen him. Tell me, was he alone there, by the stream?"

Dio shook his matted head. "No, master," he said. "There was another there, one of your own folk, in rusted gear and a broken helmet. They must have gone down together. But it is no dishonor to the Roman—he only carried an oak staff. It was not worth bringing to you, hacked and splintered as it was. We

buried them together in a grave near the stream. Did we do right, master?"

Drucus got up slowly from his stool and went toward the window. "You did right, Dio," he said. "What else could you do?"

The slave stood quietly a little while longer, then he said, "This sword, master . . . where am I to put it?"

The Roman began to move toward the doorway of the room. "Take it back to where it belongs," he said. "Lay it beside the man who held it in his hand. I refused it when he was alive; I cannot take it from him now. It is not my sword."

So Dio left his master and, being afraid of the dark, called two other slaves to go with him back to the stream with their mattocks and picks.

And as they went, looking back over their shoulders at every creaking of bough or crying of bird, Dio said to his fellows, "Our master is one of the bravest of men, yet I swear that he was weeping when I left him."

A young slave called Simia, because he was so nimble at tree climbing, said laughing, "These Romans! I do declare, I shall never understand them. You would think that they'd rejoice at the death of their enemies—yet they weep like women!"

Dio whispered softly in the dark, "We are only slaves, Simia. Perhaps we do not mean the same thing by our tears as these Romans do, after all. Perhaps they weep out of revenge."

Young Simia flung the bronze sword into the air and caught it again, very cleverly, because he could scarcely see it in the dusk.

"Yes, Dio," he said, "that must be it. Otherwise there is no sense in the world."

Then they came to the place where the sword must be buried. The moon rode from behind a cloud and showed them where to dig. It was just below a hawthorn tree. The red flowers on it looked so gay in the moonlight that young Simia broke one off and stuck it into his dark hair. Then he started one of their work songs for the others to dig better by, and it was not long before their work was done, and the sword had gone back where it belonged.

When they returned to the farm, they saw the other men working by torchlight at the new timbers, and their master, Drucus Pollio, astride the old roof ridge, blackened with soot, and flinging down the charred old thatch like a madman.

"Come, come, you lazy hounds!" he called out to them, his red face shining with sweat. "Put your backs into it and we'll have the new roof up by morning!"

The slaves who had come from burying the sword stood still, staring up in astonishment.

Dio sighed and shook his head. "I tell you, my friends," he said, "these Romans are not ordinary men. What they are, I do not know; but they are not ordinary men."

PART THREE

9

The Old Friends

THE next morning Dio felt a hand on his shoulder, shaking him. He opened his eyes and saw his master, Drucus, bending over him, already dressed in a hooded cloak of gray woolen cloth and carrying a stout oak staff in his hand.

"Do not disturb the other slaves," whispered Drucus. "What I have to say is for you alone. I am going away for a while. Look after the farm as though it were your own. Treat the men well, and see that they are fed. If I come back, you and I will share this place. If I do not come back, then the farm is yours. I have been up half the night, setting this down on a paper for you. Here it is, and together with it I have pinned the paper that will give freedom to all the slaves who work here."

He placed a tightly folded scroll in Dio's hand.

At first Dio gazed at the scroll without understanding. Then he jumped up from his straw pallet and said, "Master, we are happy as we are. We do not want to be freedmen. We want you as our father. Why are you going to leave us? Someone will come and make us slaves again, or kill us. Why are you going away?"

Drucus took Dio by the arm and led him outside, where they

would not disturb the sleepers with their talk. Then, in a quiet
voice, he said, "Dio, it is no business of yours where I go. The
less you know, the better in these strange times. Keep these
papers safely and carry on as though I were still with you. I
shall think of you. Now be a good man and forget me for the
time being. Mithras guard you."

Then Drucus turned and walked firmly away from the farm,
never once looking back. Dio watched him go until a clump of
trees hid him, then he looked down at the rolled papers and
suddenly saw that a tear had fallen onto them. He wiped his
eyes and went into the master's villa, feeling very strange and

lonely, and not at all like a man who owned half of what was there.

Drucus walked on steadily, hardly daring to think about anything but the rutted road under his feet. Once, when a wide-eyed hare came staring at him from behind a patch of foxgloves, the centurion paused a while, and, leaning on his staff, said, "Good day, comrade. We live in strange times. Don't put your nose out to sniff at every passerby—some of them may carry spears in their hands, not staffs, like me."

The hare twitched his nose and then flicked his right ear back and forth. Then he came out toward Drucus, with his head on one side, moving clumsily on his great hind legs until he was within a yard of the man's sandaled feet.

Drucus smiled down at him and whispered, "Oh, brother hare, my poor friend, why do you not take warning? There are some Romans who would have you in the cooking pot within the count of ten fingers."

He stood still, looking down at the stupid creature, smiling, trying not to make any movement that would frighten it. Then, after a while, he said gently, "Now, be off with you. I wish to walk along this path and you stand in my way. Off you go now, brother, and may Mithras keep you out of harm's way."

He raised his staff slowly, and the hare hobbled across the path and then stood staring at him from under a reed bed. Drucus went on, but looking back after ten paces, saw that the mild-eyed beast had come out again and was sitting in the path, watching him go. Now he shook the oak staff quite wildly, but the hare only sat there, gazing at him without fear.

Drucus was still thinking about this and wondering why some creatures were born mild and others fierce when he topped a small heather-covered rise and looked down on the stream that fed the cattle troughs of the next farm. It had overflowed its banks and was swirling in a way he had never seen before. So he walked a dozen paces down the slope and then saw what had dammed the water to make it do this. Men lay sprawled upon each other, their arms and legs dangling, their hair floating in the water. They wore the coarse cloth of slaves. Some of them had been shot with arrows, others pierced with spears. They were all dead.

At first, Drucus thought of trying to move some of them, so that the water would run through again to the cattle. Then he looked across the grazing field and saw the cattle lying there, some on their sides, others on their backs with their legs thrusting up, and he knew that they would not need water any more.

Almost by habit, he gazed upward toward the blue sky, and there he saw six pairs of eagles wheeling above the ruined farmstead, waiting for him to pass on. He said to them, "You waste no time, brothers, do you? Which one of you brought the news, I wonder?"

He was walking through the bedraggled corn when he almost fell headlong over a man who lay there, half hidden by the tumbled crop. It was Calgacus, still holding a scythe against his red breast. A yard away from him lay a blue-painted Celt with a bunch of heron's feathers in his dark hair. Drucus looked down on them sadly. Tears came up into his eyes, and he could not speak, even to say farewell to his old comrade.

He found Vitalis under the wall of the still-smoldering farmstead, his left hand twined in the long hair of a great-chested savage, his right hand clenched round the ash shaft of a wood ax. There were five arrows in the Roman's body, all of them driven to the feathers.

Now Drucus could go on no further. He sat in the dust beside his old friend and let the tears run down his cheeks unwiped.

And at last he shook his head and, bending forward, punched with his closed fist at the ground before him. "I swear, Mithras," he said, "I swear I will not lie down in sleep again until vengeance has been got for these two good men. I will go back to the legion and take up the sword again. I will join them as a common foot soldier. But I will join them. Hear me, Lord of Light, these two were my comrades. We marched in Germany together. We shared a cup of water in the desert of Africa. Vitalis beat the buzzards away from me when I lay sick under the walls of Antioch. And I dragged Calgacus out of the Tagus when we were ambushed there and both of us shot with arrows. My Lord, give me the strength to hold the sword again. Give me the chance to face this witch, this butcher, Boudicca. O, Mithras, give me luck!"

And when he had said this, a leaf fluttered down from an alder tree above him. It fell onto his right arm and lay there. He saw that it had turned red with the coming of autumn. It was the color of blood. He took this leaf and placed it carefully in the pouch at his belt. Then he whispered, "I thank you, Mithras. I thank you for this sign, Lord." Then he rose and, without looking at his dead friend, made his way past the smoking ruins of the farmstead and into a little sunken lane that ran away from the broad military road but which led toward Lindum all the same.

10

Lindum Colonia

T HE dusk had come down like thick, gray smoke before he reached the garrison he knew so well. Keeping away from the highroad, he stood behind a clump of hawthorns and looked up toward the city on the steep hill. Red fires were burning all along the wall-tops, and as he gazed Drucus could see men in armor parading back and forth, with spears over their shoulders, as though they were waiting for an attack.

Below the walls, down by the slow river, there was a humped cluster of huts where the street traders lived. These were smoldering and charred with fire. Nothing moved among them save stray dogs and lowing lost cattle crying to be milked.

Drucus made his way carefully along the dusty paths and over the creaking bridge toward Lindum. He swung his eyes from side to side as he went in the twilight, expecting all the time a shout, or a high scream, or a whirring arrow, from one place or another. But nothing happened. The place was dead and deserted.

Now he had got the measure of it, he strode as fast as his blistered feet would let him up the slope toward the garrison gate.

He was wondering how he would announce himself, what words he would use, when from the watchtower that over-looked the cobbled ramp a voice called loudly, "Stand and declare yourself, traveler."

Drucus stopped dead then, knowing that six arrows would be trained on him. He even felt himself smile a little as he spoke, for he had set the guard in that tower more times than he could count. He knew what manner of men would be inside it; he even thought he might know their names.

So he stood quite still and cried out in a high clear voice, so that there could be no misunderstanding, "I am Drucus Pollio, ex-centurion, commander of the First Cohort. I come to offer my services to the legate."

He waited for the great gates to grind open on their rollers. But nothing happened. Only a heavy stillness. Then suddenly

he heard a deep buzzing sound that came rapidly toward him.
He flung himself sideways into the dust, and an arrow thumped
into the spot where he had been standing only a breath's space
earlier. It struck there, still quivering, one of the thick-shafted
arrows that the Ninth was so fond of. He reached out and
snatched it, in case there was some message pierced on it. But
there was nothing, only that deathly thing, its iron head now
blunted by the hard earth. He could not understand this, and
from where he lay, shouted again, "I am Drucus Pollio, centurion, Oak Leaf from Glevum, Bronze Eagle from Deva. I demand to see the legate. Are you deaf as well as blind up there,
you lazy louts?"

This time, as the harsh whirring came at him, he had just
time to roll over when four shafts buried themselves a hand's
breadth from where he had lain.

Now he was furious. Jumping up and flinging back his cloak,
he shook his staff at the garrison tower and yelled, "I am Drucus
the centurion. Drucus, you madmen. Drucus!"

Then something hit him beside the head, so fast that he did
not hear the whine as it came to him. It was like the blow of a
hammer and he fell away from it, half senseless before he struck
the hard ground. He felt his head thump on the cobblestones
and even heard his oak staff go rolling down the road toward the
river. Then a great blackness came over him.

Before it wrapped him around completely, he shouted out,
"They have killed Vitalis and Calgacus. Can you not hear, you
fools? I come to offer my sword to the legion. I will speak to the
legate. It is my right as a Roman."

Then he fell into such a deep pit of darkness that no words
mattered. From above him, there was some frightened laughter.
Someone said, "These British are up to all the tricks. You cannot trust them. They are an old, wily folk. They take on the
names of dead centurions to get into the garrison. Aye, but we
Romans know better than to fall for that sort of trick!"

As he lay senseless in the darkness, ten more arrows thwacked into the ground about him, almost shaping his body. Only one hit him. It was the last arrow. It went through his left leg and pinned it, just above the ankle, to the earth. He was so mauled by the one which had knocked him down, he did not feel such a small wound.

11

Crippled Hawk

IT was almost dawn when Drucus opened his eyes. He tried to stand, but fell over. Then he looked down and saw the arrow. He sat back and broke the shaft well away from his leg, then drew the two pieces out, one from either side. His legs were so cold and numb, he felt no pain. He had done this many times before, for comrades who had been hit with arrows. Dimly he looked at the wound and thought that it seemed clean. He looked at the broken shaft before he threw the pieces away and saw that they had come away without leaving anything of themselves behind. He thought that with luck all might be well. The iron head had neither broken bones nor cut tendons.

Now he got up and, leaning on his staff, went down the slope away from the fortress wall. At the bottom, by the river, a bent man in gray rags came out toward him and called in a hoarse voice, "Hey, comrade, comrade! Give me the price of a meal, I beg you."

Drucus halted, balancing on his staff, and looked at the man. He was no more than forty-five, but his hair and stubbled beard were already gray. His left arm hung uselessly by his side. He wore the rough brown cowhide jerkin of a legionary's forage-kit.

Drucus said to him gently, "You speak with a Roman clip to your words. You wear a soldier's coat. Who are you, friend?"

The man said, "When I was on the strength of the Ninth, they called me Platorius Falco. I was a decurion in the Fourth Cohort. I have been pensioned off in Camulodunum for years."

Drucus said to him coldly, "Then you were in the engagement at Mai Dun, against Caradoc?"

The man shook his head. "No, sir," he said, "the Fourth Cohort did not fight there. We went across country to set an ambush at Caerwent. That was where I lost the use of my arm. I tried to stop a chariot. It was there that I first learned that Romans were not gods!"

Drucus went to him and took his hand. "You speak the truth," he said. "A liar would have claimed to have been at Mai Dun, where the fiercest fighting was. You are a true man, Falco."

The veteran shook his head and flung away a tear. "Up there, at the garrison, they do not think so. I left the colony and walked all the way here from Camulodunum to offer my services. They shot arrows at me."

The first morning light began to appear, and Drucus smiled, though his leg was beginning to throb now. "They did the same to me, and I was not without some merit in the Ninth," he said. "If we could only have spoken to the legate, instead of these nervous recruits on the walls, we should have been treated better."

Falco said thickly, "I do not think so. Petillius Cerialis is a broken man, they say. He galloped back here with a handful of cavalry. He passed me, along the road by Ancastor. I lay in a bush and watched him ride, screaming like a madman, with the British hanging onto his horse's tail and trying to get the ax to him. He will be dead by now, on his own sword, as a defeated general should die."

Drucus said faintly, "We are two old men, Falco. We have been turned away by our own regiment, in a foreign land. From now on, what soldiers do and what their generals do is no concern of ours. You asked for the price of a meal. Do you know where we might both eat such a meal?"

Falco smiled grimly and nodded. "There is a village less than five miles south of here, deep in the woods. I found it on my way up to rejoin the Ninth. The folk in that village are all Brigantes. They do not care which side a man is on as long as he has good money to pay for his board and bed. Have you money for both of us?"

Drucus began to sway on his staff. He said faintly, "Feel in my pouch, Falco. I forget what I brought with me now. Only put your good arm round me, or I shall fall. I have a slight nick in the leg that is starting to announce itself quite loudly."

Falco helped the centurion to sit on a milestone by the roadside. Then he felt the pouch, and a smile lighted up his face. "You came away with enough to see us to safety, sir," he told Drucus. "I am honored to share it with you."

Drucus felt his head nodding. "Do you know who I am, by any chance?" he asked.

Falco smiled. "I never forget a face," he said. "There was a time when I dreamed of you twice a week. You were my hero."

Drucus smiled. "Aye," he said, "and I remember you. Falco the Hawk, they called you. I recall having to speak sharply to you once, for striking a lazy infantryman with your staff."

Falco said, "He deserved it; so did I. Now times have changed, and I am a crippled hawk indeed. But I still have the use of my legs, and I think—if you feel strong enough to move now—we should be on our way. It is getting light, and we should not find much mercy from either side if we were found here, two helpless old fellows that we are."

12

The Village

IT was slow going out of Lindum town. Drucus could hardly put his foot to the ground now. But the place was deserted, except for scavenging dogs that roamed the streets, sniffing and bristling. In one small square a dozen such creatures snarled and snapped over the carcass of a horse. Others dragged at the leather tunic of a dead soldier. Drucus turned his head away in grief.

By the time the sun had heat in it, they were clear of that place of terror, but they did not dare use the straight, wide military road in case they met tribesmen. They kept mainly to the sunken lanes, overgrown with brier and hawthorn, where they would not be seen.

Once, at midday, when Drucus was resting on a stone and groaning with pain, they heard wild shouts and saw a troop of Celts riding on the skyline toward Lindum, tossing a Roman helmet from one to the other as they went.

Later on, when the centurion's thigh had began to swell and he could scarcely hobble, they saw a line of wagons in the distance and heard the war songs of the massed folk who followed them.

Falco said grimly, "The man who put the arrow into you may have need of that shaft before the day is out. He will regret having wasted it."

But Drucus could not answer. His thoughts were on getting to some quiet, safe place now, before his senses left him. Then, all at once, they breasted through a clump of beech saplings, and there below them, by a little stream and surrounded on all sides by gorse-covered slopes, they saw the village. There were only six thatched huts, but smoke rose blue from the chimney holes, and geese cackled in the fenced yards. Sheep grazed peacefully on the hillsides, and men moved about without weapons, carrying water buckets or scything the small square patches of barley.

Drucus smiled and whispered to his companion, "Mithras be praised! I cannot even feel that I have a leg now. And all from one small scratch!"

He fell forward and rolled a little way down the slope before Falco could save him.

When he woke again, it was dark outside, and he saw that he was in a place where rushlights burned in brackets on a wooden wall. A big fire blazed in the middle of the room. Falco was at one side of him, kneeling, and a red-cheeked woman with graying hair at the other. He saw that she was dressed in a blue gown and wore a big bronze brooch just below her throat. She smiled at him and said, "You are a lucky man! If the arrow had struck an inch higher, or if I had had no skill in herbs, you would never have walked again. And if it had not been a clean, well-kept Roman shaft, you would never have wakened again, Centurion."

Drucus said stiffly, "How do you know my rank, woman?"

She smiled as she wiped her hands. "In your sick dreams you have been shouting out parade-ground orders and giving commands—who could doubt what you were?"

Falco coughed and said, "Some of the words were not the

politest I have heard. It is a good thing that these folk are broad-minded."

Then they all smiled, and a little later when Drucus was drinking a cup of broth and chewing at a piece of newly baked bread, some of the young men of the village came in quietly and stood by the door to watch the Roman eat, as though it were an honor to have him in their village.

Drucus said to Falco, "You see, these are not wild savages. They are honest folk, such as we try to be. It is sad that we have turned Boudicca and her Iceni against us."

Falco frowned and said angrily, "Boudicca is a witch. Her tribe are savages; they are brutes and beasts. But these are Brigantes. They are different."

Drucus shook his head. "They are all the same, comrade," he said. "They are just human creatures. Treat them well, and they behave as the god meant them to. Treat them ill, and you can turn even the best of them into wolves."

But Falco got up and stumped to the door, growling like an angry dog. "They are all beasts, the Iceni," he kept saying. "Beasts who must be destroyed if Rome is to survive."

13

Black News

NO one came to disturb Drucus while his wound was healing. There were times, as he sat outside in the sunshine, listening to the doves cooing on the rooftops and hearing the young girls singing as they gathered the sheaves of barley, when he wished he could stay in this peaceful place for the rest of his days.

But one morning the kindly woman with the bronze brooch came to him and said seriously, "Centurion, we have heard black news. It will sadden you, but it is my duty to tell you. The tribes have burned Camulodunum to the ground and have killed all the veterans in that place. By now they will have done the same to Londinium. They have sworn to wipe out all Romans in Britain."

Drucus said slowly, "It is one thing to make a vow, but it is another to keep it. So far the Iceni have met only the Ninth Legion. It will be a different affair when the Second, the Fourteenth, and the Twentieth come and surround the tribes. Boudicca will have to deal with over fifteen thousand hard men then."

The woman said gently, "We hear that a hundred thousand

tribesmen are following her now, Centurion. The Romans will not find it easy, I fear."

Drucus turned his head away. He said in a whisper, "If three legions, led by Suetonius Paulinus, fall back before tribes, then I shall know that there is no longer any place for me on this earth. I shall be ready to go."

The woman put her hand on his arm in a friendly fashion and said, "Centurion, now I have something to say that sticks in my throat. You cannot stay here any longer. If it were for me to decide, you would be welcome for the rest of your life. But some of the young men in the village wish to join Boudicca and to gain glory in the war. Their hearts are turning against all Romans. And their fathers are now saying that if the queen comes up here again, she will wipe us out for sheltering you."

Drucus nodded and said, "We will not put you in danger, my friend and I. It is kind of you to tell us this so gently. Be good enough to pack us a little bread and goat-milk cheese in a pouch, and to give us a flask of your ale. We will make our way across the wolds while there is daylight. My leg is strong enough to carry me now."

But after they had topped the first rise from the village, Drucus leaned against an oak and said dryly, "It is one thing to walk about a farmyard; it is another to climb a hill. We shall take longer than I thought to reach my house, friend."

Falco stared back at him, hard-faced. "When I think of my old comrades lying stark in the ashes of Camulodunum," he said, "I do not complain. I have a useless arm, you a stiff leg. We are fortunate men."

Later that day, among the woodlands where they built a shelter for the night, Falco said again, "I thought that all hatred had left me, Drucus, but as we have been making our way across this lonely land, I have thought of all the men I knew at the veterans' colony. I can see them, lying dead with spears and arrows in them; men who deserved a better end. Not one of them was armed; they had given up the trade of soldiering. They must have died like sheep in a pen, unable to defend themselves."

Drucus said softly, "Try to forget it, friend. You will only torment yourself, thinking of it. What is done, is done; we cannot bring them back to life again."

Falco jumped up and punched at an oak tree with all his strength. "No," he shouted, "but we can make these British pay. We can vow vengeance on all Celts from this time onward."

Drucus rose and put his arm about the man's shoulders, drawing him away from the tree. "I think, friend," he said, "that there will be vengeance enough before long, without our help. Come, sit by the fire and eat some of this good goat-milk cheese. All rests in the hand of Mithras. Let us be patient. Let us leave it to the god who sees more than we can."

But Falco drew away from the centurion and stumbled into the wood, to let his tears flow in private.

14

The Homecoming

IT was another three days before they reached the farmstead. Dio and Simia and some of the other slaves came running to meet them, laughing and waving their hands in greeting.

"Master, oh, master," Dio said, falling to his knees, "we were afraid that we should never see you again. What have you done to your leg? Let us carry you into the house. We have kept it clean and have lighted fires in your room, waiting for you to return."

Drucus pushed him away gently, then turned to Falco and said, "These are my people, Falco. We live together as a family. They will care for you, too."

The other Roman drew back, his eyes narrow with fury. "A family!" he said. "These are not *my* family. These are British savages, of the same breed that murdered my comrades in Camulodunum. I would rather wolves cared for me than these treacherous vultures."

Dio and the slaves stood quite still and gazed at Falco, wide-eyed and bewildered. Then Simia said to Drucus, "Lord, we have never hurt anyone. You have always taught us to behave

correctly. What does the Roman lord mean? We have killed no
one."

Then Drucus put his hand on Simia's shoulder and said, "The
Roman lord means no harm. His words spring from his grief.
Look after him now, he is weary from journeying."

Simia went forward with a smile now, to help Falco into the
house. But the Roman suddenly swung around on him and
struck out with his left hand. The young slave boy staggered
back, blood trickling from his nose. The others murmured in
surprise but made no movement.

Drucus turned to Falco then and said very calmly, "That was
an unkind blow, comrade. You will regret it later, but Simia is
a good boy and he will forgive you."

Falco laughed wildly. "A savage slave will forgive me!" he
shouted. "But shall I ever forgive him and his kind for butcher-
ing my friends in Camulodunum? No, never! These are my
enemies, I spit on them all. If I had my way they would hang
from crosses. And you would hang with them, for you are as
much the enemy of Rome as they are."

That night, after Falco had calmed down and had gone to his
bed, Drucus sat by the brazier warming his hands and wondering what his duty was. He sipped at a cup of elderberry wine
spiced with cloves, which helped to drive some of the evening
chill from his bones. As he sat there, he felt very old and weary.
He thought to himself: If I had known that my life would turn
out like this, sitting by a little fire in a lonely farm, with no one
to talk to, no one but my slaves to stand beside me, I wonder
whether I would have joined the legion after all?

Then suddenly he was aware that Dio had crept in silently
and was standing beside him in the shadows. Drucus could see
that the man's face was troubled and his hands were visibly
shaking.

"What is it, old companion?" he asked gently. "Why are you
standing like that, as though you expected to get a beating from

someone? Are you not a free man now? Did I not give you that promise? Why should you shiver before any man?"

But Dio took the centurion's hand and pressed it to his forehead. "I do not wish to be free, master," he whispered. "Nor do the others. We are happy to be with you, to serve you. That is our life. We know no other life. Do not send us away."

Drucus smiled and said, "Why should I send you away? I like having you here, in the house, with me. You must know that."

The slave bowed his head, then said in a low voice, "Yes, master, we know that. Perhaps I am afraid because there is someone else in the house now, too."

Drucus sighed. "Falco will get used to our ways, friend," he said. "You must be patient with him. He is an old soldier who grieves because his comrades have been massacred. In his place, you would grieve too, Dio."

But Dio shook his dark head. "I was not speaking of Falco, master," he said. "There is another. Someone who came secretly yesterday, at nightfall. Someone who is hiding under the straw in your barn. Someone whose name I dare not mention. Will you come and see him, lord?"

Drucus took a torch from the wall bracket and followed Dio across the stackyard. In the barn, he almost fell back with surprise. Lying on the straw, fast asleep with exhaustion, was a young warrior with tawny-reddish hair, wrapped in a cloak of the same tartan Boudicca had worn. About his neck hung a bone tally on a narrow thong of leather. By his side lay a bronze sword, its blade now so bent and hacked as to be almost useless. A long gash down one cheek was caked with dried blood. One of his legs was bound with a stained bandage of coarse linen.

Drucus said in a shaking voice, "It is not Lydd Guletic, is it? How can he have come back again? How . . ."

Dio shook his head. "It is his brother, Mabon," he said. "He came knocking at the door in the darkness last night looking for

shelter. He was sickened by his tribe after the killing at Camulodunum. They tried to kill him, so he turned back here, an
outcast from his own people."

As the slave spoke, the young man's blue eyes suddenly
opened. He snatched at his sword and drew back against the
wooden wall of the barn, his bent blade held forward, his face
fierce in the torchlight.

Drucus smiled down at him and said, "Put down your sword,
Mabon. I am your friend. Your brother Lydd was my friend. We
have no war against one another."

For a while the Briton stared at him, unblinking, then slowly
he lowered the bronze sword, and at last he let it fall into the
straw as though his thin hand could not carry the weight of the
weapon any longer.

"I am your prisoner," he said. "Treat me as you will. I have
lost the heart for fighting."

Drucus looked at him sharply, then turned to Dio and said,
"He is almost dead of hunger. It is a sin for such a young eagle
to die starved in the straw like this."

Dio bowed his head. "We offered him food," he said, "but he
would not eat until the true master of this house had given him
leave." Then he added quietly, "He would not take bread from a
slave, sir."

Drucus Pollio sighed and answered, "Mithras! O Mithras! And
we think that Romans are a proud folk. When will we learn! Dio,
when will we learn?"

Dio scratched his cheek and said, "That I do not know, lord.
But I do know that if we do not get this boy into the house and
by a warm fire soon, he will die. I have seen young warriors die
for no reason, like pining hawks and falcons. This one will go
like that. See, he has given up, his face is white, his bones are
showing, he is almost a dead man."

Then Drucus Pollio stooped and took up the boy in his arms.
He grunted a bit to do this, but he laughed, too, and whispered

down to the youth, "I have a stiff leg, lad, and am not the gentlest of nurses. It is an old rheumatism that comes over me from time to time, but be patient, I shall carry you. By Mithras, in full war gear I have carried heavier trophies in my day—but none so precious. Put your hands round my neck, lad, and hang on. We'll get there, and you shall have meat and drink, and a soft bed by the fire at last. Be easy now, the worst is over."

Before Mabon Guletic's head sank down, he answered, "When my brother, Lydd, and I rode forth, Father . . ."

He was fast asleep with wounds and weariness.

The tears ran down the cheeks of Drucus. He felt them as he struggled to hoist the boy. But he still had strength enough to say to Dio, "If you ever report this, I will . . ."

Yet he did not say what he would do. Dio did not need to be told. He knew Drucus well enough. He followed with the torch, so that the lame centurion should not stumble with his new son.

15

The Twentieth

THREE mornings later, Drucus was in the far pasture with Dio, looking where a new wall might be built, if the god gave anyone the time to build a wall. The other slaves were following behind, each of them pointing out where he would put a wall, and all arguing in a quiet, happy way.

All at once, Dio, glancing toward the south, said, "Horsemen are coming to this villa, lord. The dust off the wolds is rising like fire-smoke. Can you not see it?"

Drucus stared and said, "Yes, I can see it, Dio. That dust rises from no more than twenty riders, which means that it is a forward cavalry detachment of a legion. Your own folk would come either with three horses—or three hundred."

Then he turned and said to the slaves, "Go among the rafters of the byre. Do not speak, though the flames may crackle over your heads. If I am alive when all has passed, I will call you down. You are brave men, so do as I say. Now go."

And when they had all gone silently, Dio said, "Master, if this is what I think it is, then Rome is scouring the black pot clean. You are safe enough, and so is your friend Falco—but the youth Mabon . . . they will not be gentle to him."

Drucus bent and picked up a piece of stone into which small flints were embedded. He said, "Look at this stone, Dio. This would go well, set in a wall. Very curious, very strange!" Then, more quietly, he said, "Take him with you, wherever you go, but keep him safe. I shall have my own things to do. May the luck go with you both, and if we do not meet again—why, we have not been bad friends on earth."

They looked each other in the eye, smiling, but did not shake hands. Then suddenly Drucus was left alone.

He was still alone when four tribunes with a following of horse soldiers cantered up to where he stood. The leading tribune wore red plumes in his gilded helmet and a long blue cloak that covered his white horse's rump. He laughed in the sunlight and called out, "Hey, Centurion, we heard you might be here, so we cut across country. The legion is following us, but will be a little late."

Drucus Pollio bowed to his superior officer and said, "I am honored, sir. What news have you?"

The tribune swung his leg over his horse's back and got down. He swept his eyes around the farmstead, then said, "We trapped the old witch. Just the Fourteenth and the Twentieth, you understand. The Second got pinned down at Glevum and couldn't join us."

Drucus stared at him in bewilderment. He said, "You mean to say that ten thousand of you faced her hundred thousand, sir?"

The young officer pretended to find some dust on his breast-plate. When he had gone through the motion of brushing it off, he said, "The battle was not too hard. It lasted all day, but we were in a good position, whereas she had brought all her wagons, with all the women and children, to swell her host. I doubt whether she had more than fifty thousand men, all told, with her. We had to kill them all."

Drucus felt the sweat running down his back at these words. The sun was warm on him, but his body was suddenly as cold as ice. He said, "The women and children too, sir?"

The tribune glanced at him briefly, then nodded, with a smile. "It was a little hard," he said, "but we made ourselves remember Camulodunum and Londinium and Verulamium, and all our veterans lying with their throats cut. Then we didn't seem to mind so much."

Drucus said in a low voice, "When you begin to dream, sir, in a few nights' time, you may begin to mind then."

The tribune nodded brightly and said, "Yes, perhaps, Centurion, perhaps. But at the moment, our problem is to water the horses. They won't last to Lindum. Where is the nearest stream?"

Drucus pointed toward the east, where Lydd Guletic lay buried. He did not speak. He could not speak.

The tribune saluted him with a light wave of the hand and then the detachment galloped on. The dust behind their horses' hooves smelled as sour as old blood. Drucus turned away and made his slow path back to a little spinney he had planted. He had put a stone seat there, and on this seat he eased himself down; he was very tired. He did not think about anything, he was too weary to think. He let his hands roam over the stone seat like lizards seeking warmth, sensing the smoothness and the roughness of the stone—nothing more, nothing less.

He was still sitting there when the First Cohort of the Twentieth came tramping the earth flat, off the military road, past his farmstead.

16

The Little Knife

A blunt-faced centurion strode up through the dust
to Drucus as he sat on his stone seat, rapped him lightly on the
knee, and almost shouted, "You, comrade, we are here!"

Drucus looked up gradually, then said, "Yes, your tribune told
me to expect you."

For a while the squat centurion was silent. His face got redder
and redder. Then he said, "The tribune only wanted to water his
horses. I come with a cohort for starker things."

Drucus stared the man down, then said, "If you come for food
and drink for a cohort, my friend, then you are unlucky. This is
a small farm. It only feeds two of us, two retired officers of the
Ninth."

The centurion grinned and nodded his round head. Then he
hitched off his iron helmet, walked over to the stone seat, and
sat heavily beside Drucus. The smell of the leather he wore was
very strong. He said, in a harsh voice, "We carry our own rations, Centurion. You should know that. What we are after is
redder meat. Have you any British in your house?"

Drucus waited a while before answering. Then he said carefully, "Roman, in my house there are only friends. There are none in my house who are enemies to Rome."

The soldier wiped the beads of sweat from his forehead, then smiled and said, "I am more than pleased to hear this, Drucus Pollio. You draw a pension from the Senate, so you are still a Roman. And you know how Romans feel. Our general, Suetonius, has commanded that we wipe the eastern district clean. They are all to die, so that Rome might give civilization to the others, those who did not follow Boudicca."

Drucus answered, "How did she die, their queen?"

The man said, "She died well. For a savage, she died well. When she saw that the fight was lost, she swallowed poison be-

fore we could get to her. She was a brave woman; it must be said. Now be as honest with me. Have you any Celts in your house?"

Drucus could hardly swallow, his throat was so dry. And just as he began to speak, Falco suddenly came up behind the stone seat and stood glaring down.

The centurion said again, "Have you any Celts in your house? I shall not ask a third time."

Drucus rose and moved behind the seat. He said on the way, "I told you that I had not, my friend."

When he stood behind Falco, he said even louder, "No, Centurion, Falco and I look after this farm alone."

And, as he said this, he drew from his pouch a sharp little iron knife that shepherds used when they found old ewes on the hillside, crippled with foot rot.

Falco suddenly cried, "He is lying! Centurion, it is a lie that he speaks."

Drucus quietly put that little iron blade up under Falco's ribs in his back, so that the sharp point just broke the skin. And, as he did this, he whispered, "You will die long before these soldiers kill my people, friend."

Falco turned to him with a strained smile and said, so that all should hear, "Don't push me, brother. I just want to tell the centurion the truth."

Then, as Drucus pressed the knife point forward, Falco called out, "My brother lies, you understand. We do not look after this farm alone. We have a helper. His name is Gaius Saufeius, who came with the Ninth many years ago. So old he is, his name is not on the army lists now, I would think. He is too lazy to go up to Lindum and draw his pension. But then, he was once a Greek, and you know what Greeks are!"

Drucus took the little knife away as the cohort roared with laughter over the ravaged field. Half of them were Greeks, anyway.

The centurion got back onto his square-built pony. He said sternly to Drucus, "You are not the wisest of men, for an ex-centurion, friend. What you need is a few good slaves on this place, to keep it in order. I see that your grain fields are badly trampled down. Keep them clean in future, even if you have to employ a few Britons to help you. But see that they are trustworthy, you understand."

Drucus nodded grimly as the cohort wheeled among swirls of dust and set course back to the highroad. And when they had gone a distance, he took the little knife from Falco's back and said, "I am sorry to have pressed the point so hard, my friend. It had to be done."

Falco stood upright and flexed his back again. He turned smiling and said, "No, I understand, Centurion. You need not explain to me. A farm as big as this needs men to cultivate it. You did not want to see good farm laborers killed, just for revenge. And I agree with you. That would be stupid. I can see the sense in it now."

Drucus felt his leg giving way, so he sat down on the stone seat again. Then he nodded and said, "You are right, as ever, Falco. We must keep the farm going, you and I, for without it we are beggars."

He looked around the empty plain for a while, until he knew that all the dust had settled, all the men had gone. Then he said in a new voice, "Now come with me back to the house—and meet my son."

Glossary

Alexandria, a city in Egypt.

Apollo, a very handsome Greek god, borrowed by the Romans.

Apulum in Dacia, a city in Rumania.

Ballistae, big Roman catapults, which flung rocks at the enemy.

Belgica, now Belgium, where many Celts came from to settle in Britain.

Boudicca, the one great British queen who stood against Rome. Her name means "Victorious Woman" and is the same as our "Victoria." Because of a mistake in handwriting, an early scholar set her down as "Boadicea," and the incorrect name is still often given to her.

Brigantes, a British tribe living to the north of the Humber and to the south of Scotland.

Caer Caradoc, a British hilltop fort in Shropshire.

Caerwent, an ancient British fortress town near Cardiff in southern Wales.

Camulodunum, Colchester.

Caradoc, a British king who fought against the Romans almost twenty years before Boudicca did. History books usually call him "Caractacus," though his correct Latin name was "Caratacus."

Celts, another name for the British people before the Saxons came to live in Britain.

Cohort, 600 soldiers of a legion.

Coritani, British tribes living in Lincolnshire and Nottinghamshire.

Decurion, a Roman officer with ten soldiers under his command.

Deva, Chester.

Demetae, a British tribe living in southwestern Wales.

Diana, a Roman goddess identified with the Greek Artemis and often called "the Huntress."

Druids, the priests of the early British tribes. They worshiped in oak groves.

Eburacum, the city of York where the Ninth Legion was stationed when they left Lincoln.

Ermine Street, the Roman military road from London to York.

Gaul, France.

Glevum, Gloucester.

Guletic, a Celtic title, meaning "Leader."

Iceni, a British tribe living in Norfolk and Suffolk.

Jupiter, the name which the Romans gave to the most powerful of the Greek gods, Zeus.

Legate, the commander of a legion of more than 6,000 men. In effect, a general.

Libya and *Carthage*, two big areas of North Africa.

Lindum, Lincoln, where the Ninth Legion was stationed.

Londinium, London.

Mai Dun, the Celtic name for "Maiden Castle" in Dorset; an ancient earthwork fortress, whose name means "the Big Town."

Mithras, an eastern god who was so brave that Roman soldiers prayed to him.

Nero, the cruel and stupid Roman emperor at the time.

Ostia, a seaside place near the mouth of the river Tiber on which Rome stands.

Parthia, roughly speaking, Persia.

Pylus, a town in Greece.

Quartermaster, the officer in charge of a legion's stores and equipment.

Saguntum, Sagunto, just north of Valencia on the east coast of Spain.

Senate, the Government in Rome.

Simia, a name which means "monkey" in Latin.

Suetonius Paulinus, the Roman governor of Britain at this time. He was also the supreme commander of all the legions in Britain.

Tagus, a river in what is now Portugal, which was called Lusitania in the time of Drucus Pollio.

Tarraco, Tarragona, just south of Barcelona on the east coast of
    Spain.

Tartan, the many-colored cloth by which any Celtic clan or family
    group could be recognized.

Tribunes, staff officers, below the legate, but above the centurions.
    Usually noble young men, they were sent out from Rome, and
    were not professional soldiers.

Verulamium, the present English city of St. Albans.

Veteran, a soldier who had spent his full time in a legion and was re-
    tired on a pension awarded to him by the Senate.

Villa, the Roman name for a country house.